AF406601

WHAT A BEAUTY!

Fátima Guzmán

®2022 Editorial Bien-etre.

All rights reserved. The partial or total reproduction of this material by any means or method without the written authorization of the author is prohibited.

Published by: Editorial Bien-etre.

Cover design: Mary Pérez

Editorial design: Easwara Jiménez

Illustrator: Heidy Quiñones Guzmán

Translated by: Heidy Quiñones Guzmán y Ana Villamán

ISBN: 978-9945-636-03-1

Edition: Editorial Bien-etre

www.a9Od.com

First edition 2022

What a Beauty!

Fátima
Guzmán

Dedicated to All the dreamer children.

A long time ago, on a Caribbean Island, a little girl named Luisa was born. Since the early months of pregnancy, her mother walked on the beach, and amidst laughter and seaweed that tickled her, she would let her feet get wet with the seawater while collecting sea snails to decorate the crib and the Moses basket in which the baby would sleep when she was born.

Every afternoon, the happy mother would sing to her baby in the womb, with the melody of the ocean waves playing in the background.

Luisa would be the youngest of her family.

During her birth, she did not cry, but started singing; she had eyes as green as the ocean and lips as red as a starfish. Whenever she wanted her mother to carry her in her arms, she would sing such a beautiful song that everyone would come close to hear her.

Her neighbors assured that this girl was not like the others, because she had the look of an angel and a softness in her skin that was noticeable when she was carried, since she slipped into their arms as if she were a fish. She had to be held tightly so she wouldn't fall. It was also said that in order for her to fall asleep, her mother had to give her seawater in the feeding bottle.

As Luisa grew older, her beauty became rarer. In her eyes, you could see the ocean and all its mysteries. When she sang, she did it in a language that no human had ever known.

On her birthday, Luisa was just learning to walk, and without anyone noticing or knowing how, she left the house and, in a few minutes, arrived at a nearby beach.

Even though she was small, Luisa would hide behind the trees so she wouldn't be discovered by the neighbors passing by. Without being seen, she continued her way to the beach, guided by her instinct and following the sound of the ocean, as well as the song of the mermaids inviting her to join them.

When her mother noticed she was missing, she immediately started looking for her. She begged her husband, children,
neighbors, and friends to help her find her. They all agreed
and took different paths while shouting her name. But deep
down, her mother knew that Luisa was no ordinary girl, in fact,
she looked like a mermaid, so she thought that might be the
reason she had gone straight into the sea so unexpectedly.

When she arrived at the beach, the first things she saw
were her small pink shoes and the flowered dress she had
sewn for her birthday party.

Without knowing how to swim, she desperately entered
the water, when suddenly, she heard in the distance the melodious voice of Luisa singing to her from a rock in the middle
of the sea. And being shocked by the change in her little girl,
she placed her hands on her chest, trying to catch her heart
that wanted to come out after her daughter. At that moment,
her husband arrived to keep her company, and while trying to
understand what was happening, he held her tight in his arms
to comfort her. The father also watched in awe and wonder at
the beauty that Luisa was becoming.

"Mom, mom don't cry for me. I will come to you every day and every evening you will come to me, and you will see how happy I am", Luisa sang in a melodious voice.

From then on, Luisa could never return home, because her feet transformed into a shiny and majestic fishtail; her skin grew turquoise scales, her hair also grew and changed color as it brushed against the seawater, and she turned into a beautiful mermaid.

Her siblings and friends arrived at the beach a few minutes later. From afar, they could see how beautiful she looked and how happy she felt.

Luisa had never been so full and happy. She was now swimming to the beat of the waves, her scales shimmering and changing to iridescent under the sun's rays.

As they frolicked in the water, the other mermaids surrounded her, and through beautiful songs, they showed her the charms of life in the sea. They were now her new family.

Luisa's parents and siblings were very sad to see her drifting away in the waves, but they soon realized that she was different and that her new home was in the sea.

Some friends tell the story that her mother never stopped going to the beach when the sun went down and that she felt fulfilled knowing that her daughter was enjoying her new mermaid world. Her father never understood why he had a mermaid daughter, but deep inside what mattered to him was the love he felt for her. On the other hand, her siblings admired her and thought she was the most amazing and beautiful mermaid girl who had ever existed.

Rumor has it that when you get close to the sea, keep silent and close your eyes, you can hear Luisa and her mermaid sisters singing in the distance, and it's inevitable to exclaim "What a beauty!" because her voices sound like divine angels that help you find happiness.

Finally, Luisa became an enchanting mermaid, who with her beautiful voice conquered the seas surrounding the island and was known as the most beautiful mermaid girl in the world. The island changed its name to Luisa's Island, the enchanted mermaid, whose fame spread far and wide.

With her charms, she attracted tourists and villagers, who, like her mother, waited for the sunset to meet Luisa and her mermaid friends.

Every day, the island, which seemed hidden before, became more popular and the news that a woman had had a mermaid daughter was the source of many legends; some beautiful and others full of suspense and unknowns that frightened children and had nothing to do with reality.

Luisa, with her sympathy, was a friend to all the boys and girls of the island. In the afternoons, she told them stories with the help of her siblings and offered them small concerts in which she played her favorite musical instrument, which was made with seaweed, a giant snail and the dorsal fin of a magic shark.

One day, a fisherman from another country moved to Luisa's enchanted Island. He was an albino man who had stained hands and an overwhelming appearance, his eyes hid among his white hair and his beard covered almost his entire face. The day he arrived on the island, he made everyone believe that his intention was to live off the sale of fish, so he asked what kind of fish were marketed on the island, and by promising to share his profit with the other fisher- man, he moved to a cabin close to the seashore.

But soon, the neighbors noticed that there was something strange about this man and murmured worriedly about how sus- picious it was that he was settling so close to the beach just after he heard about little Luisa. What no one knew was that this man's desire was nothing else but to get valuable infor- mation to sell to a magazine that was distributed to many countries and distant towns, and that they had a peculiar interest in such a strange and fascinating finding.

One afternoon, Luisa's mother went to see her as usual, when she heard the neighbors whispering about the mysterious man's intentions. Immediately, Luisa's mother ran frightened towards her house, leaving behind some colored pearls that she had brought to her daughter for her to wear as a precious necklace.

When she arrived home, she told her husband with a tightness in her chest that she felt Luisa was in danger and that she must stay away from the shore, so that she would not be caught in a net like a regular fish.

Luisa's father went to the beach and with a firm voice he asked: "Who is the new fisherman?".

The albino came out to meet him and introduced himself as a fishmonger expert, saying that thanks to him the island was going to be famous with all the mysteries he was going to discover. Luisa's father remained silent and immediately realized that the man had a special interest in his mermaid daughter, since she was the only one who could arouse so much curiosity on the island.

Meanwhile, like every afternoon, Luisa went to meet with her mother and when she realized that she was not there, she hid behind a rock and saw her father talking with the albino. Seeing his concerned expression, Luisa got worried and met with her mermaid sisters to make a plan in which the albino would leave the beach for good, so that she could see her mother again every sunset.

Luisa's mother was anxious, so to help her relieve her stress, she prayed to protect her daughter from all harm. Her plea pierced the heavens and reached the ears of God.

The following day, the waves were stronger than ever. The sea became more and more agitated, as if it were angry, and prevented the fishermen from casting their nets into the sea. Meanwhile, Luisa gathered all her aquatic friends to fight for the freedom of her new town, and thus prevent their lives from being disrupted by someone who wanted to expose all their secrets without thinking of the harm this will do to all the species that lived happily in the sea.

Then, at dawn, a group of mermaids led by the king of the sea, approached the shore, and lifted the waves, making a wall of multicolored water that highlighted the indescribable beauty of these special beings that adorned the beach. As Luisa looked at the beach from afar, the nostalgia for her mother made her cry and the tide rose until the fishermen on the shore decided to move away, leaving their nets, and promising never to go fishing on that side of the island again because they believed it to be enchanted by Luisa, the island's mermaid.

From that day on, Luisa became the first revolutionary mermaid who defended the freedom to live without the fear

of being captured and exhibited as an odd creature. Her mother was now able to visit her at every sunset, as she enjoyed
the new songs that Luisa would compose in the company of
her sisters.

The years went by, and although Luisa kept a beautiful
relationship with her human family, her struggle to keep the
beach free from foreigners who only visited the island for
curiosity became more difficult and dangerous for her and
her siblings. So, one day, Luisa took a white sea snail and with
colorful seaweed, she wrote a farewell letter to her mother .

Dear mother! I can't cry because my tears will raise the tide and drown you. Nor can I stay, because I put you at risk every time you come to visit me. I think the best thing to do is to go away, deep into the sea; soon I will build my own family and they will fill me up with happiness. That way I won't die of sadness for not being able to see you again. I will always talk to them about you and dad, my siblings, and every beautiful memory I keep from those years.

Remember me in the rainbow that will welcome you for me; remember me when the waves crash, when the tide wets your feet, when the moon lights up the beach and when you look at the rock where you saw me for the first time. Laugh when the seaweed tickles you, as it tangles around your feet, think of it as a flower I send you from my new home.

You will always be on my mind, mom. And the day I get married you will feel it in your heart because I will give you signs and will send you greetings with the fish. Every time you see the sunset, you will give me your blessing with a smile, and you will feel relief in your heart because you did your best.

Forever Luisa, your mermaid daughter.

Luisa's mother received the message with love, and to honor her existence and share such an incredible story, she dedicated her life to writing stories that would brighten the days of all the children in the world. She never cried again, she followed her daughter's advice and always felt her close, understanding that true bonds are those that are built from the heart.

THE END

Painting Luisa

Draw your family

Draw yourself doing
what you like the most

ABOUT THE AUTHOR

Fátima María Guzmán Gómez, was born on May 12, 1976 in the city of Moca, Espaillat Province in the Dominican Republic. She is the daughter of Silverio Guzmán and Eugenia Gómez. And mother of Adriana, Noel Adrián and Amalia.

She emigrated to Canada in 2009, the place that began her young career as a writer.

A better world is part of his contribution to society, it was his first work, inspired by his deepest longing; to turn the great Metropolis of Montreal, Quebec into a place where families have the opportunity to dream big in the midst of adversity.